My Papa Likes

David A. A...

Illustrated by Karen Yarnall

"In loving memory of my Dad "Grandpa Willie" who loved children and loved to tease."

To order additional copies of this book, contact:
Xlibris Corporation
1-888-795-4274
www.Xlibris.com
Orders@Xlibris.com

I went to visit my Papa and MomMom.
We had a sleep-over.

When I got up, my Papa made me pancakes. He asked me if I wanted an egg on top. I said, "No Papa, kids don't eat eggs on top."

Papa asked me if I wanted pickle juice with my pancakes. I said, "No Papa! Pickle juice… that's yucky!" I had orange juice instead.

After breakfast, I went outside and
started to play. I fell and scraped my
knee. I started to cry.

My MomMom said, "Next time don't run so fast, then you won't fall and get hurt."

Papa called MomMom and said...
"Quick, bring the pickle juice!"

I said, "No Papa! Pickle juice…
that's yucky!"

MomMom said, "Papa, stop teasing!" She kissed it and made it all better instead.

Papa played ball with me in the yard.

The bugs bit me hard. I told Papa the bug bites itched and guess what he said… "Quick, get the pickle juice!"

I said, "No Papa! Pickle juice...
that's yucky!"

MomMom said, "Papa, stop teasing!
Pickle juice can't fix that!" She used bug
spray instead.

After my game, I took a long nap. When I got up MomMom fixed me a snack.

My Papa came in and said, "Would you like some pickle juice with that?" I said, "No Papa! Pickle juice... that's yucky! I don't want that."

MomMom gave Papa quite a look and MomMom said, "Papa, stop teasing! He can't have pickle juice for a snack." She gave me a tall glass of milk instead.

Papa asked me to help him pick pickles from the garden. I said, "Papa, they are not pickles, they are cucumbers."

My Papa said I have a green thumb.
I like to help my Papa in the garden.

We picked a bucket full of cucumbers
and took them to MomMom. I helped her
make a big batch of pickles.

Guess what? When you make a big
batch of pickles... you have a whole lot of
pickle juice!

My Papa was really, really hot and
thirsty from working in the garden.

I called MomMom and said,
"Quick, bring the pickle juice!"

MomMom said, "Here Papa, this is what you get for teasing!"

Papa said, "No thank you. Pickle juice...
that's yucky. Let's have a cold glass of
water instead!" And we did.

CPSIA information can be obtained
at www.ICGtesting.com
Printed in the USA
BVIC01n0123211117
500981BV00012B/71